This book belongs to

_____

Magical Birthday Fairy

Written by: Maria Tracy

Illustrated by: Anastasia Moshkarina

Magical Birthday Fairy
Copyright 2020 by Maria Tracy

Author: Maria Tracy
Illustrator: Anastasia Moshkarina
Editor: Nadara Merrill

ISBN 978-1-7355685-0-8 - Softcover
ISBN 978-1-7355685-1-5 Hardcover

Magical Berry Books
Langhorne, PA
www.MagicalBerryBooks.com

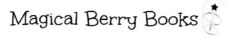

Dedicated to Lily & Luke.
Thank you for bringing magic
to every minute of my life.

M.T.

Have you ever met a magical birthday fairy? These tiny fairies live in
a beautiful garden full of flowers and silly colors everywhere!
The trees are red, the grass is yellow, and the sky is purple polka dot.

When a fairy flies past anything, the colors change.
An orange butterfly changes to a pretty pink.
Bright red rocks change to sparkling green.
The flowers change to every color of the rainbow.

Berry was a curious fairy who was always searching for a new adventure.

One day, he went exploring outside the fairy garden. He flew by an amusement park, through a big city, over the ocean, and past a zoo.

As Berry was flying around, he saw a sad little girl and boy sitting on the sidewalk in front of their house. Oh no! What could be wrong? They were twins named Lily and Luke and they had a birthday coming up. But there was a problem.

"Mom said we can't have our birthday party because Grandma's sick," Lily told her brother.

"Lily it'll be OK," Luke said.

"How? Now we won't have any fun on our birthday," Lily complained.

Berry wanted to help, but what could he do? He flew back to the fairy garden and told his friends about everything he saw while he was exploring. His friend Rosey asked, "What's the matter? Why do you look so sad?"

He told them about Lily and Luke and their cancelled birthday party.
One of the fairies said, "Maybe we can help!"
"But what can we do?" another fairy asked.
They all wondered, how could they help fix this problem?

"Maybe we could send them on a rocket ship to the moon? Wouldn't that be fun?"
"What if we take them on a trip around the world? That would be amazing!"

"Wouldn't they love to go to the jungle? What an adventure that would be!"

Berry said, "These are all great ideas, but I don't think they'd be allowed to go to the moon or the jungle or around the world."

Then Daisy, the shy little fairy, said in a quiet voice,
"Well they can't have the party, but we can still help them have
a fun birthday!"
Berry asked, "What do you have in mind, Daisy?"

Daisy said, "If we use our fairy dust, we can give them a magical birthday. We can get little treats that Berry can take to them each night. And instead of celebrating their birthday for just one day – let's do it all week long." All the fairies began cheering! They loved this idea!

So Berry flew back to Lily and Luke's house to leave a note.

Lily & Luke,
I'm your Magical Birthday Fairy!
Here to surprise you-my name is Berry!
Each night, I'll visit & bring a little treat.
Might be a tiny toy or something to eat.
So, let's enjoy this fun -filled week
Of fun & games of hide & seek.
Signed,
Berry

Lily and Luke read the note and jumped up and down with excitement! This was going to be such a fun week!

That night when their mom tucked them into bed, they couldn't stop talking about their magical birthday fairy.

"Luke, what do you think he'll bring us?" Lily asked with excitement.
"I don't know, but I can't wait to see!" Luke said.

Lily and Luke woke up each morning and dashed downstairs full of excitement to see what surprises they'd find. Every day began with a game of hide & seek, searching for their treats.

One day, they found a bag of delicious lollipops.
Another day, they got stickers they used to make crafts.
The stuffed animals were perfect to snuggle with each night,
while a big box of chalk kept them busy for hours.

Lily & Luke,
Your big day is almost here
It's so exciting-it's time to cheer!
What present are you hoping to get?
Dolls, cars, games or maybe a pet?
But remember, it's the little things
that mean the most,
Like finding a treat next to
your toast.
Signed,
Berry

Berry would sometimes leave them silly notes - they loved these, too!

The treats were never big, but they were special. Lily and Luke had the best birthday week ever!

On the last day, Berry left one more note.

Lily & Luke,
Yippity, Dippity Doo
It's your birthday - WooHoo!
Hope you enjoyed your little treats.
You deserve them - you're both so sweet.
And if your friends ever need some
birthday cheer,
We'll visit them too and come back
each year!
Happy Birthday Lily & Luke !
Signed,
Berry
Your Magical Birthday Fairy

This is the story of how Berry became a magical birthday fairy. Today, magical birthday fairies around the world bring magic to children everywhere!

SEE YOU NEXT YEAR!

BERRY

Magical
Birthday
Fairy

Personalized Letters From Berry:
 Check website or email Berry for details

WEBSITE: www.MagicalBerryBooks.com

EMAIL: MagicalBirthdayFairy@aol.com

FACEBOOK: Magical Facebook Fairy

INSTAGRAM: @Magical_Birthday_Fairy

CONTESTS: For a chance to win, post a picture
of your child with their Magical Birthday Fairy book
on social media and tag Berry.

Made in the USA
Middletown, DE
17 December 2020